Y0-AQL-953

This
book belongs
~ to ~

Published by
Borghesi & Adam Publishers Pty. Ltd.
Suite 328, The Block
98–100 Elizabeth Street
Melbourne Victoria 3000 Australia
Telephone (03) 9654 6070 Facsimile (03) 9650 2822

First published 1999
Reprinted 2001

Stories retold by Emma Borghesi

Manufactured in China

National Library of Australia
Cataloguing-in-Publication data
Scherger, Joy.
My favorite fairytales
ISBN 0 9577 403 01
ISBN 0 9577 403 28 (pb)

My Favorite FAIRYTALES

PAINTINGS BY JOY SCHERGER

Snow White and the 7 Dwarfs

Contents

For Holly and Bridgette

and to the everlasting wonder of children

Sleeping
Beauty

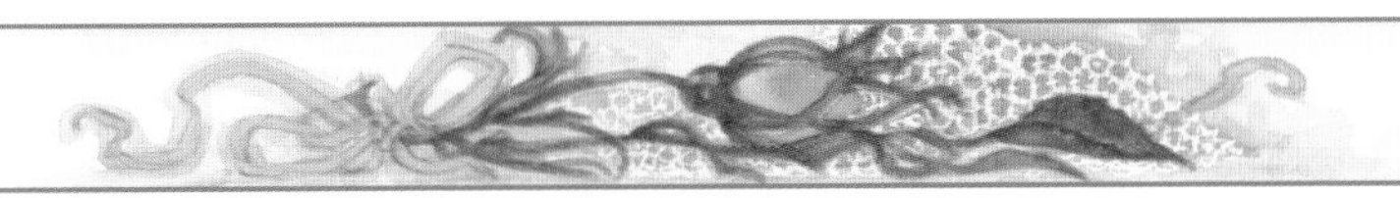

Once there was a King and Queen who were very happy, but more than anything in the world they wanted a child of their own. At last, their wish was granted and a baby princess was born.

'We must christen her and welcome her into the world,' said the King. 'We shall invite all the good people in the kingdom to attend.' And so the next day the christening was held at the palace.

Among the guests were twelve fairies who lived in a nearby forest. But there was a thirteenth fairy who was old and bad-tempered and who was not invited. Many years ago, she had argued with the other fairies, and had wandered off on her own. Everyone had long since forgotten about her.

The old fairy heard about the christening and was very angry. 'How dare they not invite me!' she muttered. 'I shall have my revenge!' Then she crept up to the palace and watched the christening take place.

Inside, each of the fairies was making a special wish. 'I wish for the baby princess that she grows to be good and kind,' said the first fairy. 'I wish for the baby princess to be filled with grace and beauty,' said the second. 'I wish for the baby princess to love and to be loved by all who know her,' said the third. And so it continued, until it seemed that all the fairies had finished.

Then suddenly the old fairy stepped forward from behind a pillar. 'Ha!' she cackled. 'I wish for the princess that on her seventeenth birthday she shall prick her finger on a spindle and die!'

The King and Queen fainted with horror and there was much distress in the palace. The old fairy crept away, smiling to herself as she thought of the sadness she had brought to the occasion.

But there was one small fairy who had not yet made her wish. 'I cannot undo the old fairy's spell,' she said, 'but I can make it less harmful. And so I wish now that when the princess pricks her finger she shall simply fall asleep and shall not die.' Everyone sighed with relief, but still the King and Queen were anxious, and so the King ordered his men to destroy all the spindles in the kingdom.

The years passed happily, and the baby grew to be a beautiful young girl. She played in the palace and in the nearby village, and was loved by everyone whom she met.

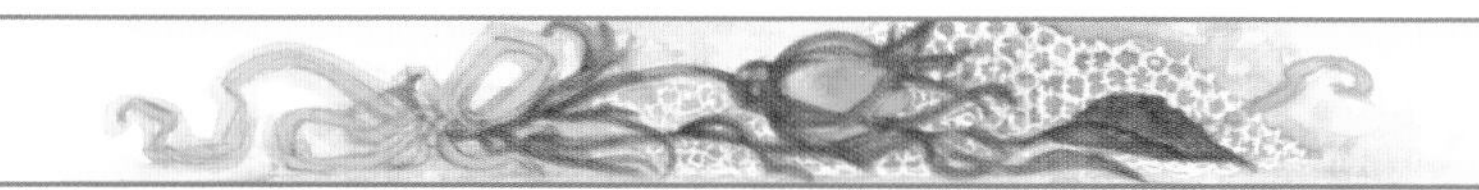

On the day of her seventeenth birthday, she went for a walk around the palace and came upon a small door in a tower which she had never seen before. She pushed it open, and found herself at the base of an old wooden staircase.'I wonder what lies above,' she thought, and so she climbed the stairs and came to a small room at the top. Inside sat an old lady spinning. 'What are you doing?' asked the princess, for she had never seen a spindle.

'I am spinning,' said the old lady. 'Come and see.' So the princess stepped forward, and she was so fascinated by the spindle that she reached out to touch it. As she did so, she pricked her finger on one of its spokes.

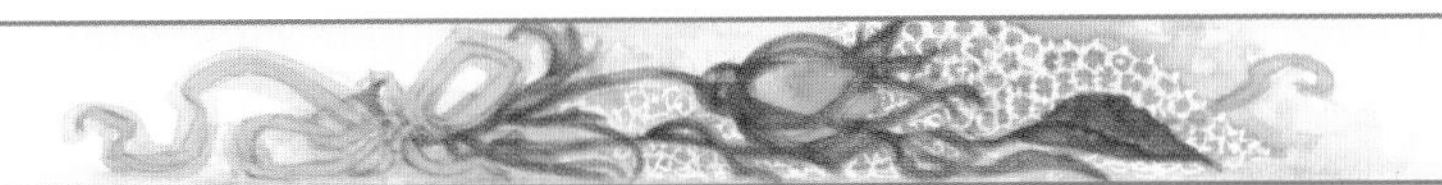

'Oh!' she exclaimed. 'I have hurt my finger!' Then she hurried down the stairs and back to the palace. Soon, she began to feel unwell, and fell into a deep sleep from which no-one could awaken her. At nightfall, the King and Queen and all their servants went to sleep, and hoped that she would awake by morning. But once they closed their eyes, they too fell into a deep sleep.

The years passed, and still no-one awoke. A thicket of rose bushes grew up around the palace walls and grew so high that the palace was hidden from view. The bushes were so thick and the thorns so sharp that no-one could pass through to the palace inside. A hundred years passed, and still no-one inside awoke.

One day, a prince arrived at the village. He had heard about a princess who had been asleep for one hundred years, and he had come to see if it were true. The villagers told him, yes, it was true, but that it was too dangerous for him to try to pass through the bushes to reach the palace.

'I shall try,' said the prince. 'I believe a princess who shall be my bride lies beyond these palace walls.' Then he rode up to the bushes and reached out to touch one of the roses. As he did so, a magical thing happened, and a path through the thicket opened up before him and led him to the palace.

The prince rode around the palace to see what he could find. He came to the window of the princess's room, and saw before him the beautiful princess lying on her bed. At first, he thought she was dead, but then he saw that her cheeks were soft pink like roses, and that she was breathing quietly.

The prince dismounted, and found his way into the palace and to the room of the princess. So beautiful was she that he immediately fell in love. 'I hope you shall awaken soon,' he said, as he leaned over and gently kissed her.

No sooner had he done so than the princess awoke. She opened her eyes, and looked into the prince's eyes, and fell in love with him.At that moment, so too did the King and Queen and all the servants awake from their sleep. They were amazed to find that 100 years had passed, but nothing else seemed to have changed.

The King and Queen were very pleased to meet the prince. Preparations were made for a wedding, and the prince and princess were married in a beautiful ceremony at the palace.The twelve good fairies attended, for they live for one thousand years or more. But the wicked old fairy did not come, for at the very moment the princess awoke the old fairy herself had died. And so the prince and princess lived happily ever after.

Rapunzel

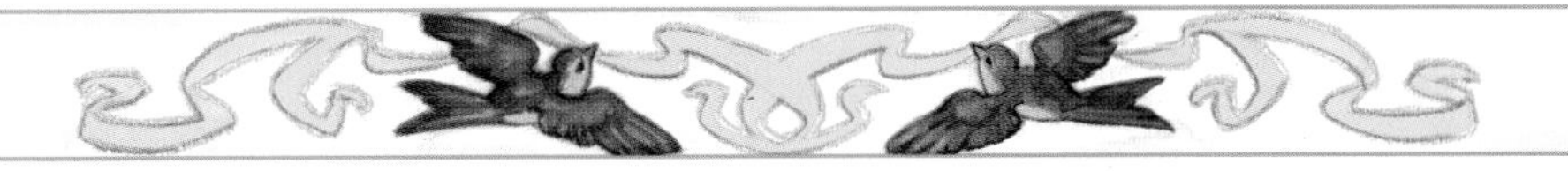

There was once a husband and wife who were sad because they had no children. Then one day, they knew their luck had changed, for within a year they were to have a baby of their own. They were very excited by this good news, and their hearts were filled with joy.

At the back of their cottage was a window which overlooked a glorious garden filled with beautiful flowers, the ripest fruit and the most delicious vegetables. It belonged to a witch, and nobody dared to enter. As the months passed, the wife sat by the window and waited for the arrival of her baby. She gazed at the garden and longed to eat the endive that she could see growing there.

'Oh,' she said to her husband. 'Please would you fetch me some endive for my dinner?' 'My love,' replied her husband, 'you know I dare not take any, for fear of the witch's wrath should she catch me.'

The wife was disappointed, and her cravings grew stronger and stronger until she felt that

if she did not have some endive soon she would die. Her husband was alarmed to see her so unwell, and so when he thought no-one was about he jumped into the witch's garden and scooped up some endive. He took it home to his wife and immediately upon eating it the colour returned to her cheeks and she began to feel much better.

Alas, the next day she became unwell again, and so that night the husband crept once more into the witch's garden to fetch some endive. This time, the witch was waiting.

'How dare you steal my endive!' she roared. The poor husband was very frightened and begged for her forgiveness.

'I know why you stole my endive,' said the witch. 'You may take what you need, but on one condition. You must hand your baby to me when she is born, for me to raise as my own.' The man was so frightened that he agreed, then he hurried back to his wife.

As the months passed,the wife grew strong on the endive and at last gave birth to a daughter. But the witch had not forgotten the promise, and soon arrived to take the baby away. 'I shall call her Rapunzel,' said the

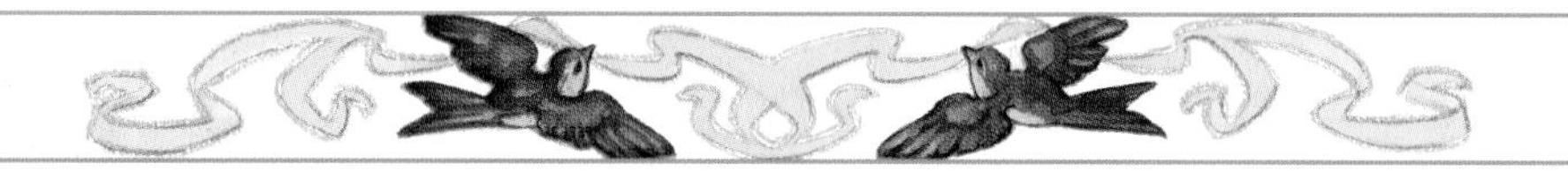

witch as the husband and wife farewelled their baby. 'Do not fear, she is in good care.'

Rapunzel grew to be a beautiful young girl. She had long golden hair which she braided into a plait that hung down her back and trailed behind her when she walked. But the witch grew afraid she would run away, so when Rapunzel was twelve she locked her in the top of a tower. The tower had no entry except for one small window at the top.When the witch wanted to enter, she would stand beneath the window and shout, 'Rapunzel, Rapunzel, let down your hair!' Then Rapunzel would toss her plait out the window and the witch would scramble up it and climb in through the window.

One day, a prince was riding nearby when he heard a beautiful song. He followed the

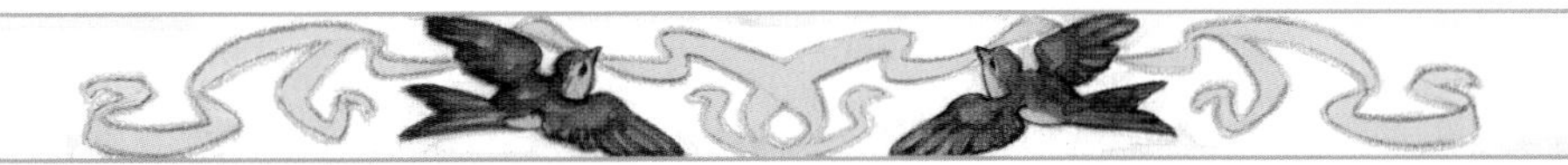

sound, and soon found himself at the base of the tower, but he could find no way to enter. At last, he gave up, but vowed to come back to try again soon.

The next day, he went back to the tower, but he saw the witch arrive just before him. He watched as she scrambled up Rapunzel's plait into the tower, and he thought Rapunzel was the most beautiful girl he had ever seen.

He returned to the tower the next morning. 'Rapunzel, Rapunzel, let down your hair,' he called, just as he had seen the witch do the day before. Sure enough, Rapunzel tossed her plait out the window, and the prince climbed up it and into the tower.

The prince loved Rapunzel from the moment he met her, and asked her to be his wife. She agreed, thinking that life with a prince would surely be better than life with a witch, and together they planned her escape. The prince would bring lengths of silk to her each day from which she would make a ladder. It would eventually be long enough to reach the ground below, so that Rapunzel could climb down to her freedom.

So the weeks passed and each day Rapunzel had two visitors. She kept the prince's visits

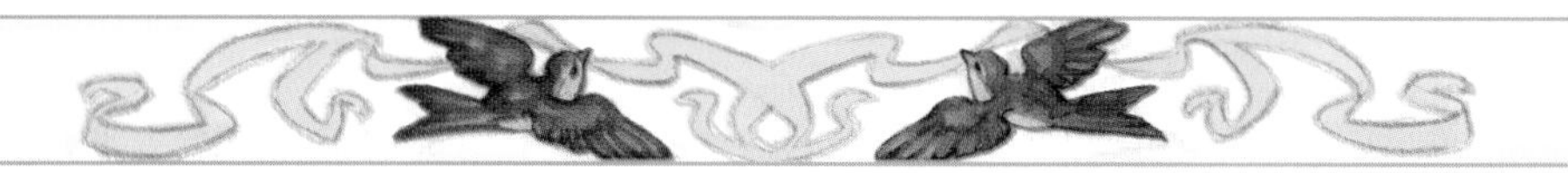

a secret until one day she made a careless mistake. 'Oh, witch, why is it that when you climb my hair you feel heavy and my head aches, but when the prince climbs my hair he is light and my head feels no pain at all?'

'What! You have deceived me!' shrieked the witch. Then she grabbed a pair of shears and hacked off Rapunzel's plait so it fell to the floor. Then she used her magic to banish Rapunzel to a barren, lonely place.

The next day the prince called to Rapunzel as usual. This time the witch was waiting, and she tied the plait to a hook then tossed it out the window so he would climb up it.

'Rapunzel has gone!' cackled the witch as he entered the tower. 'You shall never see her

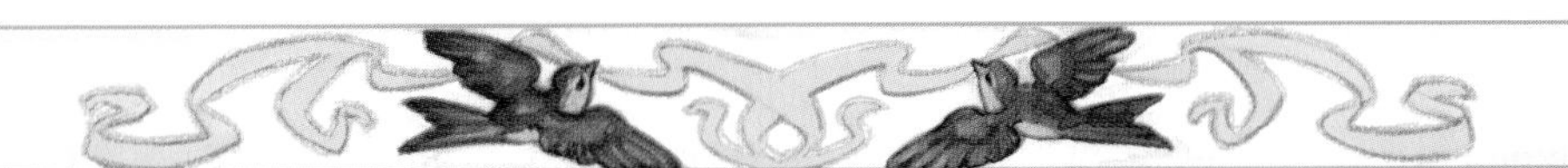

again.' The heartbroken prince was so upset that he stepped backwards and fell out the window to the ground below. Some rose bushes cushioned his fall, but two thorns pierced his eyes and made him blind.

The prince stumbled into the forest where he wandered in darkness for many years, feeding only on the berries and other fruits of the forest. He wandered on, until one day he eventually reached the barren place to which the witch had banished Rapunzel.

There was Rapunzel, singing softly to pass the time. Her hair had grown once more and hung down past her ankles, and she was more beautiful than ever. The prince heard her singing, and knew it was the voice of his lovely Rapunzel, but he could not see her and thought he was going mad.

But when Rapunzel saw the prince, she recognized him instantly. She ran towards him and took him in her arms, crying with joy. As her tears ran from her eyes and down her cheeks, two drops fell into his eyes, and his sight was magically restored.

Overcome with joy, the prince took her back to his kingdom where they were married and lived happily ever after.

Cinderella

Once there was a young girl who lived with her stepmother and her two ugly stepsisters. The stepsisters were very bossy, and made her work all day long.

Dressed in old clothes that no-one wanted, she would cook and clean from morning until late at night.Then, because she had no bed, she would curl up in the ashes of the fireplace and go to sleep. In the morning, she would be covered in cinders, and so everyone called her Cinderella.

One day, a messenger arrived from the palace. 'You are invited to the palace ball tomorrow night,' he declared. 'It is hoped that there the Prince shall meet his future bride.'

'Oh, goodness!' twittered the ugly stepsisters. 'We shall be honoured to meet the Prince!'

'May I go, too?' asked Cinderella, pausing from her sweeping for a moment.

'You?' scorned the stepsisters. 'With your face black with soot and your hair full of ash? You are not fit to meet the Prince!'

Cinderella was so disappointed that she could hardly hold back her tears. Still, she was a kind soul, and so the next day she washed and curled her stepsisters' hair, and dressed them in fine clothes which she herself had made.

At last, they were ready, and Cinderella watched as they set off for the ball. Then she picked up a broom and tried to continue her sweeping. But it was no use. She could not work. She flung down the broom and plopped herself beside the fireplace, and covered her beautiful face with her hands. Then she wept and wept. After a moment, a fairy appeared before her. Cinderella was startled. 'Who are you?' she asked. 'Why are you here?'

'I am your Fairy Godmother,' replied the fairy. 'Fetch me a pumpkin, and two lumps of sugar, and soon you shall be on your way to the ball.' Cinderella did as she was asked, and returned quickly with the pumpkin and some sugar.

'These shall do nicely,' said the fairy. Then she waved her wand once over the sugar and three times over Cinderella. Cinderella looked down and saw her ragged clothes had gone and in their place was a beautiful gown made of the finest silks. Her lovely hair tumbled down around her shoulders but was kept in place with a diamond tiara. On her feet she wore a dainty pair of glass slippers.

'Now for the coach,' said the fairy. She waved her wand over the pumpkin then over two mice whom she saw hiding under the table. 'Look outside,' she said to Cinderella. Cinderella did so, and saw a horse and coach waiting to take her to the ball.

'Be sure you are home by midnight,' said the fairy, 'for then your clothes shall return to rags, and the horse and coach shall be a pumpkin and two mice once more.' Then Cinderella thanked the fairy and hurried away to the ball.

When she arrived, she drew many admiring gasps from the other guests. Who was this beautiful girl, and where did she come from?

The prince danced with her for hours, and with no-one else again that evening. 'Surely she shall be his bride,' murmured the other guests, and while many were disappointed that they could not dance with the prince, they all agreed she would make a beautiful princess of whom they would all be proud.

Time was passing quickly, and Cinderella did not realise how late it was becoming. Then suddenly she heard the palace clock begin to chime the hour of midnight. 'I must leave now!' she cried, and without another word she fled. But it was too late. Just as she reached her horse and coach they turned into a pumpkin and two mice before her eyes, and she was dressed in rags once more. So she and the mice walked sadly all the way home.

The distraught prince ran after her, but she had disappeared into the night. On the steps, he found a glass slipper that had fallen from her foot. He picked it up gently and proclaimed, 'When I find the girl whose foot this slipper fits, I shall know I have found my bride.'

The next day the prince's knights knocked at all the homes in the kingdom and invited all the young ladies to try on the slipper. When they reached the home of Cinderella, the ugly stepsisters pushed forward to try it on.

‘There! It fits!’ squealed one stepsister triumphantly, as she squeezed her foot into the dainty shoe. But the slipper was much too tight, and her foot was red with pain.

‘I'm sorry,’ said the knight, ‘your foot is too big.’

'Let me try!’ squawked the other stepsister, snatching the slipper and placing it on her boney foot. ‘There! It fits!’ she laughed, as she pointed her foot proudly at the knight. ‘Now you can take me to meet the prince.’

‘I'm sorry,’ said the knight. ‘Your foot is too thin, and the slipper would surely fall off as soon as you took your first step.’

‘Bah!’ said the stepsisters bad-temperedly. ‘Be off with you then! You shall find no-one whose foot is a better fit than ours!’

‘But there is one girl who has yet to try on this slipper,’ said the knight and he beckoned to Cinderella. So while her stepsisters snorted with scorn, Cinderella tried on the slipper ~ and it was a perfect fit! ‘You must come with me to the palace,’ said the knight. So Cinderella took his arm and, without a backward glance, departed for the palace. There she met with the prince, and they were married the next day and lived happily ever after.

The Frog Prince

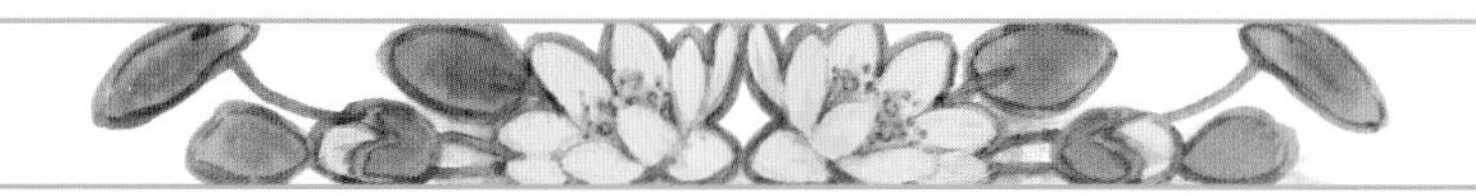

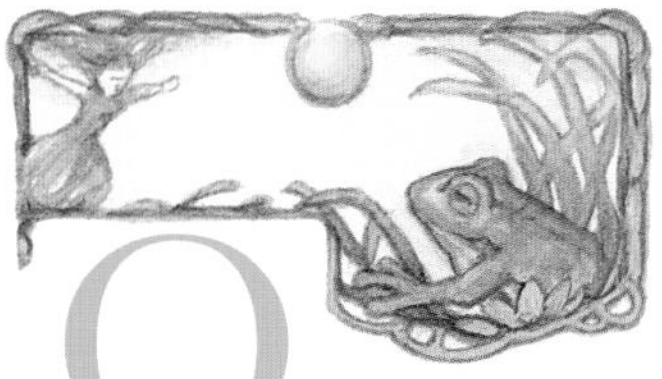

Once there was a lovely princess who lived in a beautiful castle near a lake. She was the youngest of three sisters, and the King and Queen loved her very much.

She had many beautiful jewels and wonderful fine clothes, but of all these things, she valued most of all her precious golden ball. Often she would play with it in the garden, throwing it up in the air and catching it, and rolling it along the ground and watching it gleam and sparkle in the sun. There was nothing which she treasured more.

One day, the ball rolled out of her hands and down a garden path. The princess ran after it, but it gathered speed as it rolled down a hill. She ran as fast as she could, but the ball rolled faster still, and disappeared with a splash into the lake at the bottom of the garden.

'Oh no,' cried the princess tearfully. 'My precious golden ball! I fear it is lost to me forever.' She stood by the edge of the lake and looked into its depths, but she could not

see it anywhere. So she sat down beside the lake and began to cry.

'Grrmp! Excuse me,' croaked a voice nearby. The princess raised her head to see where the voice had come from, but she could see nobody. 'Grrmp!' croaked the voice again. 'I'm over here, on the lake.'

The princess looked over to the lake, and there to her astonishment she saw a frog sitting on a lilypad. 'I am sorry to see you are so sad,' croaked the frog. 'What can I do to make things better for you?'

'Oh, Frog!' said the princess. 'I am sure I can not imagine what you could do to make me happy again. Unless, of course, you can find my golden ball...'

'I know where it is and I would be pleased to fetch it,' croaked the frog, 'but first you must promise to be my friend. You must allow me to dine with you and to sleep on your pillow, and you must kiss me goodnight before you go to sleep. That is all I ask in return.'

The princess thought about this for a moment, and decided very quickly that she did not want the frog to be her friend. Still, she wanted her ball back, and so she replied, 'Of course, dear

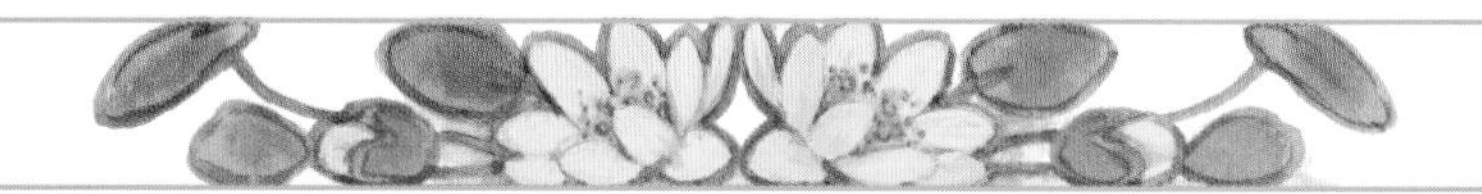

Frog. Fetch me my ball and we shall be friends for ever more.'

And so the frog jumped off his lilypad and dived into the lake. A few minutes later, he surfaced again, holding the ball in his webbed foot. The princess reached over and took it from him, and examined it so she could be sure there was no damage. Then she jumped up quickly and ran back to the palace.

'Wait! Wait for me!' croaked the frog, leaping as fast as he could behind her. 'You must not forget your promise!'

But the princess did not care about the promise. She only cared for the ball, and it was

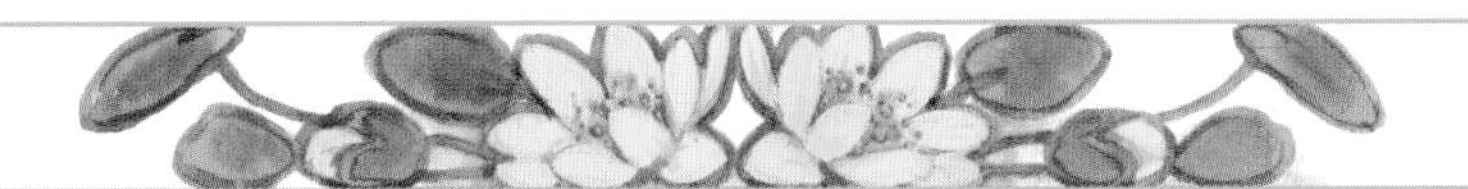

safely back in her hands once more. The poor frog tried to catch up with her, but he could only leap in little jumps, and so the princess quickly disappeared into the distance.

That night, the princess sat down at the grand dining table with her sisters, the Queen and the King. They were about to begin their dinner, when they heard someone knock at their door. A few moments later, a footman appeared at the doorway. 'There is a visitor here for the youngest princess,' he announced. 'He insists upon seeing her now!'

'Well, who is it?' boomed the King. 'Who wishes to visit my daughter this evening?'

'Grrmp!' croaked a voice from beyond the doorway. 'It is me, the frog from the lake in your garden.' Then, with a splish-sploshing sound, the frog walked into the dining room and up to the youngest princess.

'Go away, you nasty creature,' shrieked the princess. She tried to push him away, but the frog insisted on telling everyone his story.

The King listened, and was very disappointed and upset to find his daughter had not kept her promise. 'Daughter,' he said sternly, 'no child of mine shall break a promise. You must

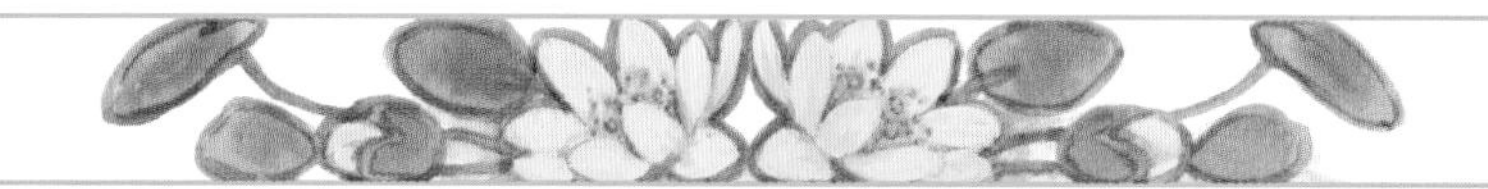

allow this frog to dine with us. Tonight, he may sleep on your pillow, and you must kiss him goodnight as you promised.'

So the frog jumped up onto the table and perched beside the princess's plate. He dined with them that evening, and when it was time for them all to go to bed, he splish-sploshed his way behind the princess to her bedroom. Once in the bedroom he jumped onto the princess's pillow and made himself comfortable. The princess was terrified, and closed her eyes tight so she could not see him as she climbed into her bed.

'Princess,' croaked the frog, 'remember you must kiss me before you go to sleep.'

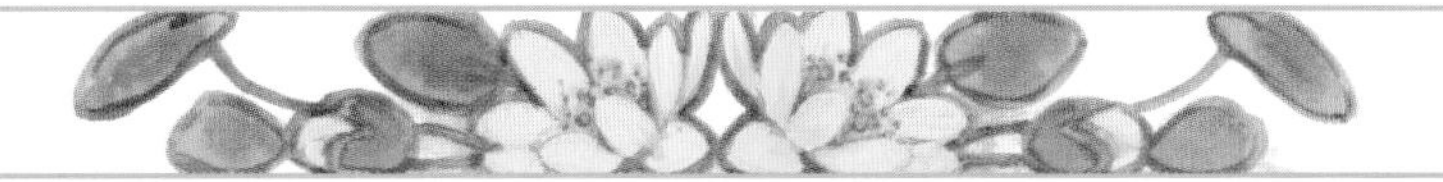

The princess tried to ignore him, but she could not, and at last she realised that if she was to have any sleep at all she would have to do as the frog asked. So, she gathered all her courage, then took a deep breath and leaned forward and kissed the frog. She then moved quickly away to the other side of the bed and went to sleep.

When she awoke in the morning she was amazed to find that the frog had turned into a handsome prince. 'Many years ago a curse was placed upon me,' explained the prince. 'I was turned into a frog by a wicked fairy, and the only way I could become a prince again was by persuading a princess to kiss me.'

He paused for a moment, and then he took the princess's hand in his own. 'Thank you for making me a prince once more,' he said. 'I had become very tired of living in the lake.'

The princess was still very cross because she had been made to sleep and dine beside the frog. Still, as the months passed, she and the prince became good friends, and eventually they fell in love.

The following spring, they were married, and their many guests included the frogs who had lived with the frog prince in the lake.

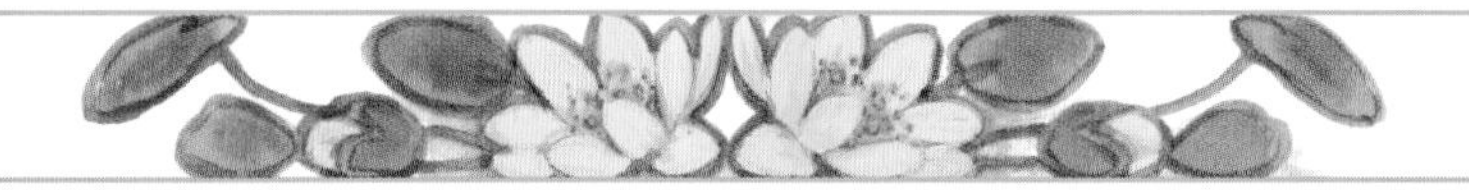

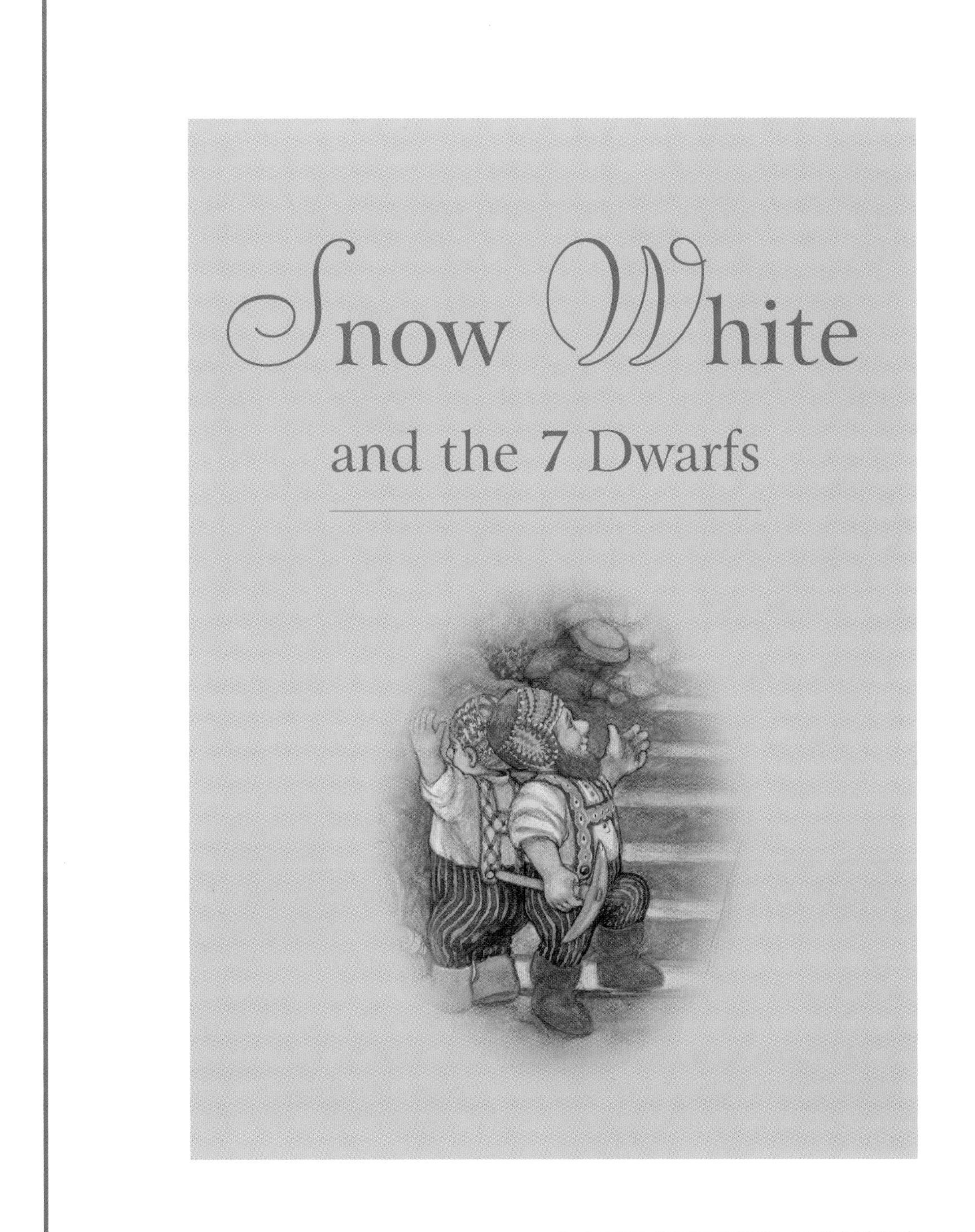

Snow White

and the 7 Dwarfs

Once there was a Queen who longed for a daughter. One day, as she sat by a window with her needlework, she pricked her finger and drew blood. 'Oh,' she said, as a drop of deep red blood fell on her work. 'How I long for a daughter who is as white as snow, as red as blood, and as black as ebony.'

The Queen's wish was granted, and soon after a baby girl was born with skin as white as snow, hair as black as ebony, and lips the colour of blood. The Queen named her Snow White, and not long after, the Queen died.

A year passed, and the King remarried. The new Queen was a wicked, vain woman, and in her room was a large mirror into which she would gaze and admire her beauty. Every morning and every night, she would ask the mirror the same question:

'Mirror, mirror, on the wall,
Who is the fairest of them all?'

And every morning the mirror replied:

'Royal Queen, you are the fairest of them all.'

SCHERGER

But as the years passed, Snow White grew more and more beautiful and the wicked Queen became very jealous. Yet each day the mirror told her she was still the fairest of them all, until one day when the mirror gave a new reply:

'Royal Queen, forgive my reply,
There is one much fairer, I cannot lie,
It is not you, Royal Queen, not you anymore,
It is now Snow White who is fairest of all.'

'What!' shrieked the wicked Queen, who was filled with rage and wished Snow White dead. She ordered a huntsman to take Snow White into the woods and to kill her, and to return with her heart so she knew she was dead.

The huntsman did not want to do this evil deed, but he had to obey the Queen. So he led Snow White into the woods, but when the time came to kill her he could not do it. 'Run away, Snow White,' he whispered. 'Your stepmother is wicked and wants you dead.' Then on his way back to the palace he killed a wild beast and took its heart to the Queen and told her it was the heart of Snow White.

Meanwhile, Snow White wandered further and further into the depths of the woods. Eventually she came upon a stone cottage. 'I am tired and hungry,' she thought to herself. 'Perhaps I can rest here.' So she knocked on the door,

but no-one answered. After a while,she stepped inside, and lay down on a bed to rest.

When evening fell, the owners of the cottage returned from their day's work. They were seven dwarfs who worked in a nearby mine. Of course, they were very surprised to find a child asleep in their home. 'What a beautiful child,' they agreed. 'Why is she here?'

Snow White woke up at the sound of their voices, and at first she was very frightened. But she soon realised they were good and kind and that they would be able to help her.

'You may stay with us, Snow White,' they said, after she had told them her story. 'If you prepare our meals and keep our home clean and tidy you shall never want for anything.'

'Oh, thank you,' said Snow White. 'I would be happy to take care of you and your home.' So Snow White lived happily in the cottage with the dwarfs, and grew more beautiful each year. But the dwarfs knew that one day the wicked Queen would find her, and so they warned her to be careful.

The dwarfs were right. Every morning and every night, the Queen consulted her mirror, and every morning and every night the mirror told her that Snow White was still the fairest of them all. The Queen could not believe what she heard. How could Snow White still be alive, and where was she? She searched the kingdom high and low, but she could not find her. The Queen grew angrier and more jealous each day, and her beauty began to fade as her anger and jealousy consumed her. One day, she shrieked at her mirror in rage:

'Mirror, mirror, on the wall,
Look what has become of me!
Where is Snow White, she must be killed
So once more the fairest I shall be!'

And so at last the mirror agreed to tell the Queen where Snow White was living in the woods. 'Ha!' cackled the Queen. 'I shall find her now.' Then she dressed herself as an old lady selling fruit, and set off into the woods.

Eventually, she reached the dwarfs' cottage.

'I am just an old lady and I mean you no harm,' she croaked in an old woman's voice when Snow White answered her knock. 'Please let me in and taste the fruit I have brought you.'

'I'm sorry,' said Snow White, 'but I cannot let you in.'

'Oh, very well,' said the Queen, 'but perhaps you would like to taste this apple,' and she held up a poisoned apple. It was a deep rich red and seemed the juiciest apple Snow White had ever seen. Still, she was frightened, and so she would not taste it.

'Look, I shall taste it myself,' said the Queen, taking a bite, but she was cunning and had only poisoned one half of the apple, and ate only from the half which she knew was safe.

Snow White watched the old lady eating the apple. When she saw that it did the old lady no harm, she could resist it no longer. She took the apple herself and bit into it. Immediately she fell down dead to the ground, and the wicked Queen ran back to the palace.

That night when the dwarfs returned from their day's work they found Snow White lying dead on the floor of their cottage. They were heartbroken, and for three whole days and

three whole nights they cried with grief, and tried to bring her back to life. At the end of three days, they believed Snow White was lost to them forever, and that they must bury her.

The dwarfs thought Snow White was too beautiful to bury in the ground, and so instead they built her a glass coffin. They placed her in the coffin and she looked as beautiful as ever. They carried the coffin to the top of a mountain, and took turns to guard it.

One day, a prince was riding through the woods and he came across the coffin. He looked inside and saw Snow White lying there. He asked the dwarf on guard who she was, and so the dwarf told him her story.

'But she is so beautiful, I want to take her back to my palace,' pleaded the prince.

'Oh, no,' said the dwarf. 'We shall watch over Snow White forever.'

'But I love her,' said the prince. 'I will take care of her, and you may visit her whenever you wish.'

His voice was filled with such sadness and he seemed so good and so kind that the dwarf at last agreed to his request.

That night, the seven dwarfs helped the prince carry the coffin down the mountain.

As they were making their way down the mountain, one of the dwarfs tripped on a rock and caused them to drop the coffin. It fell to the ground and the lid slid off.

As it did so, Snow White sat up suddenly and coughed, and out fell a piece of the poison apple which had been lodged in her throat. 'My goodness!' she said. 'Where have I been and what has happened?'

The dwarfs and the prince were overjoyed to see that Snow White was alive once more. The prince took her hand and asked her if she would marry him, and she happily said yes.

Soon, it was the day of the wedding and all the dwarfs were in attendance when Snow White married the prince. The wicked Queen had been invited to the wedding ~ for no-one knew it was she who had tried to kill Snow White ~ but when she saw that Snow White was the prince's bride she was so overcome with rage, hatred and fury that she fell down dead at the steps of the palace.

Snow White and the prince lived happily ever after, and the dwarfs often came to have tea with them at the palace.

Jack and the Beanstalk

Once there was a poor woman who lived with her only son, Jack. Their one possession was a cow, and early each morning they milked the cow and sold the milk at the market.

One year, the cow became ill and gave no more milk. They had no means to make any money, and so the woman told Jack to sell the cow so they could buy some food.

So Jack went to the market and tried to sell the cow, but no-one wanted it. He had almost given up trying when a man approached him, carrying a handful of beans.

'My good sir, give me your cow and you may take these beans,' he said to Jack. 'They are fine beans and shall bring you good fortune.' In desperation, Jack gave the man the cow and took the beans, then wandered home.

When he arrived home, his mother became very upset. 'You silly boy,' she cried. 'What use are these beans? They shall not feed us and make us strong!'

Then she tossed them out the window, and that night she and Jack went to bed without dinner.

In the morning, Jack saw to his surprise that an enormous beanstalk had sprung from the spot to where his mother had thrown the beans. It reached high into the sky and disappeared into the clouds above.

'Where does it finish?' thought Jack to himself, as he began to climb the beanstalk. Up and up he climbed, until the earth became very small beneath him and he could barely make out his home. At last, he passed through the clouds and arrived at a magical land. There before him stood a magnificent castle.

'I wonder who lives there,' thought Jack as he made his way to the castle. He knocked on the door and within a few moments an old woman answered. 'Hello,' said Jack, 'I wonder if you could give me some food?'

'Little boy, you are not safe here,' said the old woman. 'My husband is a giant, and he will want you for his breakfast. You must hurry back to the place from where you came.'

'But first you must give me some food!' pleaded Jack. So the old woman took pity on

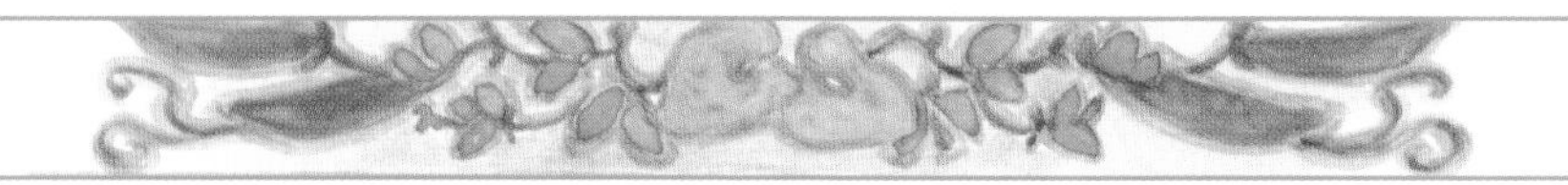

him and ushered him into the kitchen where she began to prepare some food. Suddenly, they heard heavy footsteps making their way down the passage to the kitchen.

'Hide!' ordered the old woman. 'The giant is heading this way.' So Jack jumped into a cupboard just as the giant walked in.

'Fee Fi Fo Fum, I smell the blood of an English one!' he boomed to his wife.

'Oh, no,' said his wife. 'It is only last night's supper that you can smell.' So the giant was reassured and sat down to eat his breakfast. When he was finished he ordered his wife to bring him his magic hen. His wife did as she was asked, and sat the hen down before him.

'Lay!' boomed the giant, and sure enough the hen laid an egg. But it was no ordinary egg; it was a beautiful golden egg. Jack, watching through a crack in the cupboard, could not believe his eyes. He knew the hen would be the answer to all his mother's problems.

After a while, the giant fell asleep and Jack saw his chance. He crept quietly around the table and snatched the hen, then fled back to the beanstalk. Once he was home, he sat the hen on his mother's table.

'Lay!' he said to the hen, and sure enough the hen produced a golden egg. Jack and his mother knew that they would never want for anything ever again.

As the months wore on, Jack began to wonder what other magic lay beyond the clouds. So he climbed the beanstalk once more and returned to the castle. The old lady did not recognise him, and once again she let him into the castle when he asked for food.

Once again, the giant came into the kitchen to eat his breakfast, and Jack hid in the cupboard. This time, when the giant had finished, he went to another room and returned with a golden harp. He played it for a while, and Jack was amazed that he could play so well. A sweet

melody sprung from the harp, and Jack wanted it for his mother.

After a while, the giant put the harp away and placed his head on the table and went to sleep. Jack saw his chance. He crept over to where the giant had placed the harp and took it, but as he ran to the door the harp betrayed him:

'Master, Master, help me!' called the harp. The giant woke up and was red with rage when he saw Jack stealing the harp. He lunged after him, but Jack was nimble and he ran as fast as he could back to the beanstalk.

The giant ran after him, and while he could not run fast he could take big steps, and so he very nearly caught him Luckily for Jack, the giant tripped over a rock, and this gave Jack just enough time to scramble down the beanstalk, calling for his mother all the way, 'Mother, Mother, fetch me my axe!'

When he reached the bottom, Jack looked up and there was the giant, making his way down the beanstalk in great, lumbering strides. Jack grabbed the axe from his mother, and with one huge swipe he cut the beanstalk down and it came crashing to the ground.The giant crashed into a nearby river and sank to the bottom, and was never seen or heard of again.

Goldilocks

and the 3 Bears

There was once a young girl who lived on the edge of an old forest. Her hair tumbled over her shoulders and shone gold in the sun, and so everyone called her Goldilocks.

One morning, Goldilocks went for a walk in the forest and became lost. 'What shall I do?' she thought. 'I cannot find my way home alone.' So she walked for a while longer and eventually she came upon a small cottage nestled amongst the trees.

'Perhaps the people who live here will show me my way home,' thought Goldilocks. So she knocked on the door but there was no answer. She tried again and put her ear to the door, but she could not hear a sound. It was as quiet and still as the morning.

So Goldilocks gave the door a gentle push. It creaked on its hinges and opened a few inches, so Goldilocks peeped inside. But still she could not see anyone.

'I shall have to wait,' she thought as she pushed the door wide open. There she found

a cosy sitting room with a wooden table in the middle upon which sat three bowls.

'Something smells delicious,' thought Goldilocks. So she went over to the table and looked in the biggest bowl and saw it was full of porridge. 'Mmmm!' she said. 'This is just what I need for breakfast!' Then she scooped out a mouthful of porridge and tasted it.

'Ouch!' she said. 'This porridge is much too hot! I can't eat that!' So next she tried the porridge in the middle-sized bowl beside it.

'Ooh!' she exclaimed. 'This porridge is much too sweet! I can't eat that!' And so last of all she tasted the porridge in the smallest bowl.

'Mmmm,' she said happily. 'This porridge is not too hot and not too sweet. It's *just* right.' So she took another mouthful, then another and another until it was all gone. Then she decided to sit and wait for the owners of the cottage to come home.

She sat down in the biggest chair in the room and tried to make herself comfortable. It was made of dark wood, and had a big, high back. She wiggled and squirmed, and leant forward and back, but the chair just didn't feel right.

'This chair is much too hard! I can't sit here!' she said. So she jumped off and sat in the middle-sized chair instead. It was a rocking chair, with a low back and fluffy cushions. She plumped up the cushions and rocked for a while, but still she didn't feel right.

'This chair is much too soft! I can't sit here!' she complained. So last of all she tried the smallest chair in the room. It was a pretty chair, painted white and with just one cushion. It wasn't too high or too low or too soft or too hard.

'This chair is *just* right,' said Goldilocks. 'I shall sit here quietly for a while.' But suddenly there was a loud cracking sound. Goldilocks was too heavy for the chair, and its legs had given

way beneath her. 'Oh no!' she exclaimed. 'I hope the people who live here will not be too cross with me!'

Then she climbed upstairs and lay down on a very big bed, but it was much too hard. Next she tried the middle-sized bed, but it was too soft. Last of all, she tried the smallest bed and it felt just right. She snuggled down and pulled the covers up around her ears and fell asleep.

Meanwhile, a family of bears had just returned to their cottage. They hung up their coats then went to the table to eat their breakfast. It was then they realised something was wrong.

'Who's been eating my porridge?' roared Father Bear in a big, loud voice. 'Who's been eating my porridge?' asked Mother Bear in a high, shrill voice. 'And who's been eating my porridge?' squealed Baby Bear. 'It's all gone!' Then to their surprise they saw their chairs had also been moved.

'Who's been sitting in my chair?' roared Father Bear. 'Who's been sitting in *my* chair?' asked Mother Bear. 'And who's been sitting in my chair?' squealed Baby Bear. 'Who ever it was has broken it!'

So the bears went upstairs to see what other damage had been done, and there they found

that their beds too had been disturbed. 'Who's been sleeping in my bed?' roared Father Bear, who was now very angry. 'And who's been sleeping in *my* bed?' asked Mother Bear crossly. 'And who's been sleeping in my bed?' squealed Baby Bear excitedly. 'Who ever it is is still there!'

His loud squeal woke Goldilocks up. She sat bolt upright and saw the three angry bears looking down at her. She got a terrible fright and jumped out of the bed and fled down the stairs. She ran and ran and did not once look behind her until she was safely home, and she never went into the forest again.

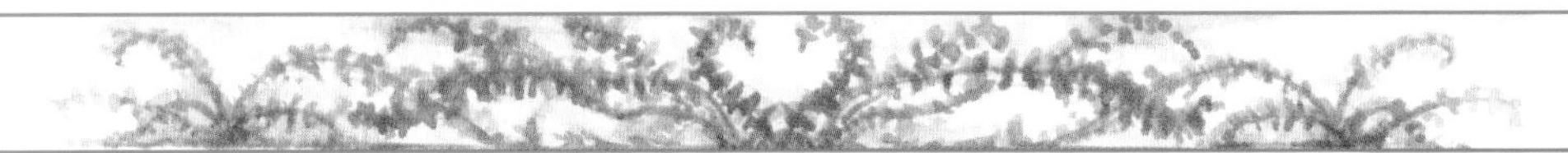